What Did You Bring?

by Daisy Ellsworth

Illustrated by Nancy W. Stevenson

Featuring Jim Henson's Sesame Street Muppets

A SESAME STREET/GOLDEN PRESS BOOK
Published by Western Publishing Company, Inc.
in conjunction with Children's Television Workshop.

© 1980 Children's Television Workshop. Muppet characters © 1980 Muppets, Inc. All rights
reserved. Printed in U.S.A. SESAME STREET® and the SESAME STREET SIGN are
trademarks and service marks of Children's Television Workshop. GOLDEN®, GOLDEN BOOKS®
and GOLDEN PRESS® are trademarks of Western Publishing Company, Inc. No part of this
book may be reproduced or copied in any form without written permission from the publisher.
Library of Congress Catalog Card Number: 79-57466   ISBN 0-307-11603-4

Big Bird sat on the steps of 123 Sesame Street. He was watching the traffic. He watched the cars and trucks going up the street. He watched the cars and trucks going down the street. But most of all he watched the cars and trucks that stopped to make deliveries. And do you know why?

Big Bird was waiting for something very special—
a present from Granny Bird. He wondered how it
would come.

Was the present in that red station wagon?
No. The red station wagon was full of dog biscuits
for Barkley.

Was the present in that blue van? No. The blue
van was bringing six clean green capes to the Count.
"1, 2, 3, 4, 5, 6...six clean green capes," said
the Count. "Wonderful!"

Was the present in that bakery truck or that dairy truck?

The driver of the bakery truck opened the back door and took out loaves of bread. A delicious smell came wafting out of the truck.

The driver of the dairy truck opened the back door and took out a case of milk cartons. Cold air came blowing out of the back of the truck.

The bread and milk were for Mr. Hooper's store, not for Big Bird. So Big Bird went on watching.

At noon a delivery girl on a bicycle arrived with a large, flat box that was tied up with string.

"Maybe Granny is sending me a very big record with my favorite bird calls on it," thought Big Bird.

But the very big record was really a pizza with bananas and anchovies for Oscar.

A bag of dog biscuits, six clean capes, loaves of bread, cartons of milk, a pizza with bananas and anchovies—there were many deliveries that morning, but no present from Granny Bird.

That afternoon more trucks came to Sesame Street.

A van from the flower shop brought flowers to Frazzle, who was sick in bed.

An ice cream truck brought ice cream.
And something that Big Bird had never seen before
came in a pickup truck. It was a present for Grover.
Grover had never seen anything like it before, either.

A moving van delivered furniture.

A dump truck unloaded dirt.

But no cars or trucks were stopping in front of
123 Sesame Street.

A tow truck passed by, taking one old car to
a garage for repairs.

An auto carrier was delivering four new cars to an automobile showroom.

And a truck pulling a horse trailer was taking Rodeo Rosie and her horse to the rodeo.

Flowers, ice cream, sculpture, furniture, dirt, cars, horses—there were many deliveries that afternoon, but still no present from Granny Bird.

Then along came a mail truck.
But the mail carrier was not delivering mail.
She was picking it up.

Just when Big Bird was beginning to think that
Granny Bird might have forgotten to send his present—
although Granny Bird never forgot important things
like presents—a parcel post truck arrived.

Now, Big Bird knew that parcel post trucks deliver
packages, and he also knew that many packages are presents.
Would it be a small package? Would it be a large package?
Would it rattle if you shook it?
Big Bird walked up to the driver of the parcel post truck.
"Do you have a package for someone named Big Bird?"
he asked.

"No, I'm sorry," said the driver. "I have a package for someone named Ernie and I have a package for someone named Bert. But there's no package here for anyone by the name of Big Bird."

"Thanks, anyway," said Big Bird. "I guess my package is coming in a different kind of truck."

Ernie and Bert opened their packages and tried on the things they had ordered—a Super-Grover secret decoder ring and a new pigeon T-shirt.

Big Bird plopped down next to Oscar's trash can.

Oscar poked his head out. "Can't you read?" he cried. "The sign says GO AWAY."

"Oh, hi, Oscar," said Big Bird. "I'm just waiting for a present from Granny Bird."

"Maybe your present is in that great-looking truck behind you," said Oscar.

Big Bird looked around and saw a garbage truck behind him.

"Oscar, do you think Granny Bird would send me a present in a garbage truck?" asked Big Bird.

"If I were sending you a present, I'd send it in a garbage truck," said Oscar. "But I never send anybody anything. Heh, heh, heh."

Big Bird walked over to the garbage collector.
"Excuse me, sir. Do you have...er, uh...
a package for someone named Big Bird?"
"All we have is garbage," said the garbage
collector. "And we garbage collectors don't deliver
garbage. We take it away."
Just then a taxi cab drove up behind the
garbage truck.

Out of the taxi cab stepped Granny Bird!
"Here is your present, Big Bird," she said.
"I decided to bring it myself!"

That night, as Granny tucked him into his nest,
Big Bird said, "Gee, Granny, I love my Teddy Bird.
And I'm so happy you came to visit me. A visit
from Granny is the very best present of all."